EGMONT

We bring stories to life

This edition published in Great Britain 2012 by Dean,
an imprint of Egmont UK Limited
239 Kensington High Street, London W8 6SA

Thomas the Tank Engine & Friends™

CREATED BY BRITT ALLCROFT

Based on the Railway Series by the Reverend W Awdry

HiT entertainment

ISBN 978 0 6035 6672 1
51283/1
Printed in China

Thomas and the Sticky Toffee

Based on *The Railway Series* by The Rev. W. Awdry

It was summertime on the Island of Sodor.

Thomas was very excited. The children were having a fancy dress party.

There was a lot to do before the party and the engines were very busy.

Percy collected the cakes and buns.

Toby collected some sticky toffee, so that the children could make sticky toffee apples!

Thomas' job was to carry the tables and chairs for the party.

When Thomas delivered the tables and chairs, he saw the children making fancy dress costumes.

"That looks like fun!" peeped Thomas.

The Fat Controller spoke to Thomas. "Thomas, I would like you to give train rides at the party," he said. "But first you must go to the Washdown so you look your best."

Thomas was delighted. He loved taking the children on train rides. But as he raced to the Washdown, he couldn't stop thinking about the children and their fancy dress costumes.

"I want to go to the party in fancy dress, too," whistled Thomas. "Then, I will really look my best."

At the Washdown, Thomas was soon covered in big, soapy bubbles. His crew scrubbed and rubbed him . . . and scrubbed and rubbed him some more.

Then, Percy arrived at the Washdown. "You look like a giant bubble!" he laughed.

"That's it!" chuffed Thomas. "I'll go to the party as a giant bubble!" And Thomas puffed away quickly, still covered in bubbles!

Thomas couldn't wait to show the children his fancy dress. He whooshed away excitedly in a hurry to get to the party.

But then there was trouble.

The bubbles flew into his eyes! Thomas couldn't see where he was going . . .

CRASH! Thomas bumped straight into the back of Toby.

"Sorry, Toby!" called Thomas. But now Toby's axle was broken!

When The Fat Controller arrived, he wasn't happy. "Toby, you must go to the Yard to be repaired," he boomed.

"But if I don't take the toffee to the party, the children won't be able to make toffee apples," moaned Toby.

"Please, Sir," peeped Thomas. He wanted to help.
"I could take the sticky toffee to the party."

"Very well," huffed The Fat Controller. "But no more
engines in fancy dress!"

Soon, all the soap and bubbles were cleaned off
Thomas and he puffed away towards the party.

"I must get the sticky toffee to the children on time," he wheeshed.

Thomas started thinking about his fancy dress costume again . . .

He thought about it for a very long time . . .

"Oh, no! I've been daydreaming!" he whistled. "And now I am going to be late."

Thomas steamed off as fast as he could. But he wasn't looking where he was going. He didn't notice that the points had changed!

Thomas bumped into the siding and biffed into the buffers. His wheels wobbled on the rails.

And sticky toffee splattered everywhere!

"Oh no! I can't give the children train rides – I am so messy," moaned Thomas. "If only I had been thinking about what I was doing."

Suddenly, Thomas saw an old branch line. "A short cut!" he peeped. "If I go that way, I can still get the sticky toffee to the party on time!"

Thomas puffed along the old line. It hadn't been used for a very long time.

Trees hung over the track and the bushes were overgrown. Thomas puffed along carefully.

Thomas bumped through the bushes and bashed through the brambles . . . but he was still covered in sticky toffee.

Something very funny was happening to Thomas. Leaves and twigs were getting stuck to the sweet, sticky goo!

But still Thomas hurried along. "Must get to the party! Must get to the party!" he puffed.

Finally, Thomas arrived at the party.

Poor Thomas!

He was covered in twigs and leaves from funnel to footplate. Only his face peeped through all the greenery!

"I've brought the toffee," he called to the children, sadly. "But I am too messy to give you train rides."

The children cheered and clapped when they saw Thomas.

"You're not messy. You're just in fancy dress! You look the best of all!" they said.

Thomas smiled happily. He felt much better now.

The children had fun at the party, and so did Sticky Toffee Thomas!